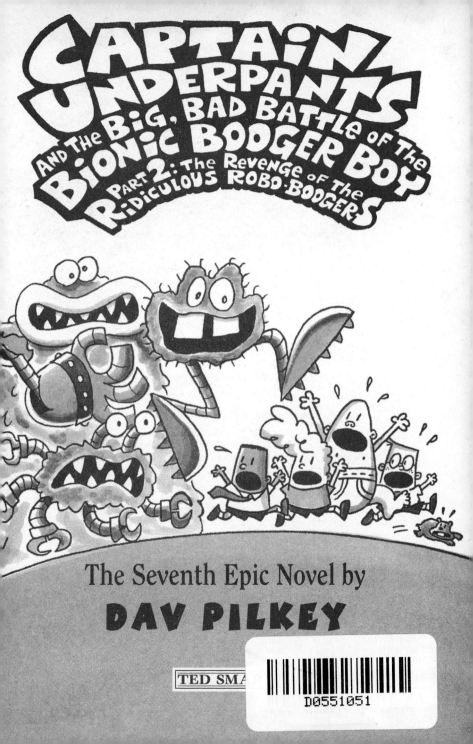

CAPTAIN UNDERPANTS

AND THE BIG, BAD BATTLE OF THE BIONIC BOOGER BOY

PART 2: THE REVENGE OF THE RIDICULOUS ROBO-BOOGERS

The Seventh Epic Novel by

DAV PILKEY

TED SMA

This edition produced for the Book People Ltd,
Hall Wood Avenue, Haydock, St Helens WA11 9UL

First published in the US by Scholastic Inc., 2003
First published in the UK by Scholastic Ltd, 2004

ISBN 0 439 95411 8

Printed and bound by Nørhaven Paperback A/S, Denmark

Be sure to check out Dav Pilkey's
Extra-Crunchy Web Site O'Fun at
www.pilkey.com

FOR AIDAN AND AUDREY HAMLIN

CHAPTERS

CHAPTER 1

GEORGE AND HAROLD

This is George Beard and Harold Hutchins.
George is the kid on the left with the tie
and the flat-top. Harold is the one on the
right with the T-shirt and the bad haircut.
Remember that now.

This is Mr Krupp, Melvin Sneedly and Sulu the Bionic Hamster. Mr Krupp is the one on the left with the underwear and the bald head. Melvin is the one on the right with the bow tie and the glasses. And Sulu the Bionic Hamster is the hamstery-looking one in the middle with the laser eyeballs, the Macro-Hydraulic Jump-A-Tronic legs, the Super-Somgobulating mini-Automo-Arms, the virtually indestructible Flexo-Growmonic endoskeleton, and the Twin Turbo-3000 SP5 Kung-Fu Titanium/Lithium Alloy Processor. Remember that now, too.

And these are the Ridiculous Robo-Boogers. Three of the vilest, most disgusting and most terrifying creatures ever to drip across the face of the Earth. Even their *names* were horrible, monstrous monikers, the sound of which would drive madness into the hearts of the bravest of heroes.

If you dare to know their nightmarishly deplorable names, I will tell you. But don't blame me if you have to sleep with a night-light on for the rest of your life.

Their names were (from left to right) Carl, Trixie and Frankenbooger.

See? I told you they were scary names!

Carl, Trixie and Frankenbooger each bellowed out terrifying, ear-piercing screams of unstoppable fury as they chased our heroes down the city streets. Finally, the Robo-Boogers cornered everyone in a dead-end alley. The three phlegmish fiends oozed closer and closer, until at last they leaped towards their prey.

The situation had become so frightening that George, Harold, Melvin and Mr Krupp closed their eyes tightly and waited for the terrifying sounds of their own inevitable demise.

GLoBBle! GLoBBle! GLoBBle!

But instead of hearing inevitable-demisey-type sounds, our heroes heard something quite diferent. You see, at the very last second, Sulu the Bionic Hamster stretched open his Flexo-Growmonic jaw and shoved the three boogery behemoths into his mouth.

Sulu's bionic cheeks swelled to capacity as he raised his furry head towards the sky.

Then, with the force of a lunar shuttle
lift-off, Sulu shot the three slimy villains
into space.

SPIT-TOOIE! SPIT-TOOIE! SPIT-TOOIE!

The three Ridiculous Robo-Boogers sailed
through the sky like cannonballs. In no time
at all, they left Earth's atmosphere and began
sailing towards Uranus. The terrifying battle
was over.

"Wow, that was a really quick story," said
Harold. "This is going to be our shortest
adventure ever!"

"Ain't *that* the truth!" said George.

CHAPTER 2
IT AIN'T

Unfortunately for George and Harold, their adventure had only just begun. As everyone walked back to school, a confusing argument got underway.

"I want my hamster back," said Mr Krupp.

"*Your* hamster?" said George. "First of all, he's *OUR* hamster now. And second of all, he never belonged to you. He belonged to Melvin."

"I don't care WHO he belongs to," Melvin interrupted. "Hamsters aren't allowed in school . . . especially not in MY SCHOOL! I'm giving all three of you bubs a detention for bringing that furry beast into your classroom!"

"You can't give us a detention," said Harold. "You're just a kid like us!"

Suddenly, Mr and Mrs Sneedly came running towards them.

"Melvin, you're all right!" cried Mrs Sneedly.

"We're so happy you're safe, son!" cried Mr Sneedly.

"Mummy! Poppa!" cried Mr Krupp. He dashed over to Melvin's parents with open arms. The sight of a bald, grown man in his underwear running towards them made Mrs Sneedly scream in horror.

"Hey, what's the big idea?" yelled Mr Sneedly.

"It's me, Poppa," cried Mr Krupp. "Don't you recognize your own son?"

"Get away from us, you – you – you
WEIRDO!" Mrs Sneedly yelled as she hit
Mr Krupp with her handbag.

Melvin ignored the commotion as he
walked past them all and went into
the school.

Melvin stormed upstairs and headed for the school office. Everyone except Miss Anthrope had already gone home for the day, and she was getting ready to leave, too.

"*Just where do you think you're going, woman?!!?*" shouted Melvin.

Miss Anthrope turned and stared in shock at the fourth grader standing behind her.

"What did you JUST *SAY*?!!?" she cried
in a voice that was rapidly becoming a
scream. "Who – WHO DO YOU THINK
YOU ARE?!!?"

"I'm the guy who's gonna fire you if
you don't get me my coffee . . . *NOW*!"
yelled Melvin.

Normally, school secretaries don't have the authority to hang a child from a coat hook by his underwear, but today had been a particularly stressful day for Miss Anthrope. She had been covered in snot, carried through town by a rampaging robotic monster and (worst of all) forced to chaperone an elementary school field trip. Now it was payback time.

CHAPTER 3

MR MELVIN AND KRUPPY THE KID

Miss Anthrope collected her things and left for home, grumbling under her breath as she passed George and Harold in the hallway. The two boys could hear Melvin's angry shouts coming from down the hall, so they went to the office to investigate.

While they were getting Melvin off the hook, Mr Krupp ran into the office, sweaty and out of breath.

"You guys have gotta help me," he cried. "My mum and dad are trying to kill me! Has the world gone MAD?"

"Relax, Einstein," said George calmly, "and put on some clothes!" George and Harold had already figured out what was going on, so they tried to explain the situation to Melvin and Mr Krupp.

"You see," said Harold, "after you guys got morphed together by the Combine-O-Tron 2000, we switched the batteries around and separated you. But for some strange reason, it switched your *brains* around. Now Mr Krupp's brain is inside Melvin's body, and Melvin's brain is inside Mr Krupp's body."

"That's a buncha BUNK!" yelled Melvin.

"Take a look and see for yourselves," said George. He pulled a full-length mirror in front of Mr Krupp and Melvin. They looked at themselves in astonishment.

"I'm – I'm a kid again," said the guy who looked like Melvin but had Mr Krupp's brain.

"And I'm old and fat and bald and ugly," cried the guy who looked like Mr Krupp but had Melvin's brain. "And I have bad breath ad cre py n se hairs and—"

"HE ell the guy who looked like ha Krupp's brain.

At this point, you might be saying to yourself, "Dang, this book is getting confusing!" Now don't worry, this'll all get cleared up by the end of chapter 17. But for now, let's rename the two characters who have the right brains in the wrong bodies, shall we? Let's call the guy who looks like Mr. Krupp (but has Melvin Sneedly's brain) "Mr Melvin". And we'll call the kid who looks like Melvin Sneedly (but has Mr Krupp's brain) "Kruppy the Kid".

Please refer to the handy X-ray chart below in case you get mixed-up:

CHAPTER 4

THINGS GET WORSE

Kruppy the Kid climbed up into his chair and demanded to know what was going to be done about this mix-up.

"I could solve this problem right away if I still had my Combine-O-Tron 2000," said Mr Melvin sheepishly, "but it got smashed in the last book."

"Well start building a new one, bub!" shouted Kruppy the Kid.

"OK," whined Mr Melvin, "but it'll take about six months."

"SIX MONTHS?!!?" screamed Kruppy the Kid. "I can't go around looking like a kid for six months! I've got a school to run, buster!"

"Sorry," Mr Melvin whimpered, "but building a cellular combiner is extremely difficult. It takes time. It's not easy like building a robot, or a time machine, or a Photo-Atomic Trans-Somgobulating Yectofantriplutoniczanziptomiser."

"Hey, wait a second," said George. "Did you just say that building a time machine was *easy*?"

"Yeah," said Mr Melvin. "It just takes a day or two. Why?"

"Well, why don't you just build a time machine?" asked George. "Then you can go back in time to before the Combine-O-Tron 2000 got smashed, grab it, and bring it back to the present time."

Mr Melvin thought for a moment, and then his eyes lit up. "I've got it!" he said, snapping his fingers. "I'll build a time machine, then go back in time to before the Combine-O-Tron 2000 got smashed, grab it, and bring it back to the – hey, what the heck is *HE* doing?!!?"

Everyone turned and looked at Kruppy
the Kid, who had just stripped down to his
underwear and was now tying a red curtain
around his neck.

"OH, NO!" screamed George. "GET
SOME WATER!!! GET SOME WATER!!!"

41

Harold ran out to the drinking fountain,
but he was too late. Kruppy the Kid shouted
a triumphant "Tra-La-Laaaaa!", then turned
and flew out the window.

CHAPTER 5
THINGS GET WORSER

"Did – did you guys just see that?" cried Mr Melvin. "I just – I mean, Kruppy the Kid just flew out the window! He FLEW!"

"Yeah, we know," said George with a sigh.

"That's – that's *amazing*!" cried Mr Melvin. "He must think he's Captain Underpants or something. Or . . . or could it be? Could our principal really BE Captain Underpants?"

"Well, *duh*!" said Harold.

"But Mr Krupp doesn't look anything like Captain Underpants," said Mr Melvin frantically. "Captain Underpants is bald! And Mr Krupp usually has hair. Hey! I know! Maybe Mr Krupp wears a toupee?"

"I thought you were supposed to be in the 'gifted' stream," said George.

"But – but how can he fly? Where did he get his super powers?" asked Mr Melvin.

"It's a long story," said Harold.

Mr Melvin calmed down a bit, walked confidently across the room, and sat in the principal's chair. He leaned back and smiled a devilish grin. "Well, why don't you go ahead and tell me all about it?" said Mr Melvin. "I've got all the time in the world!"

CHAPTER 6

THINGS GET WORSEREST

George and Harold had no choice but to
come clean. They told Mr Melvin the whole
story of Captain Underpants: how they had
hypnotized Mr Krupp, how he drank the
alien Super Power Juice, and how his super
powers must have somehow got transferred
into Melvin's body along with Mr Krupp's
brain.

While George and Harold were talking,
the smile on Mr Melvin's face grew wider
and wider, and eviler and eviler.

"What're you smiling about?" said George.
"This is SERIOUS!"

"Yeah," said Harold. "We're all in
big trouble if we don't switch
things back to normal!"

"Correction," said Mr Melvin. "*YOU* guys are in big trouble. All my troubles are OVER. I, Melvin Sneedly, am gonna get back into my old body, but KEEP those super powers for myself. I'm gonna become the world's first super-powered kid!"

"Hey, you can't do that," said Harold.

"*I can do whatever I want,*" snapped Mr Melvin. "I'm in charge now. I look just like the principal, so I'm gonna make the rules, and you guys are gonna follow them – or else!"

"Or else what?" George demanded.

"Or *else*," snarled Mr Melvin, "I'll order your teachers to give you guys twelve hours of homework every night for the next eight years!"

That shut George and Harold up.

Mr Melvin's first order of the day was for George and Harold to make a new comic book about the world's first super-powered kid, Melvin Sneedly.

"Give me a really cool name," said Mr Melvin, "like *Big Melvin* or *Mystery Melvin*..."

"MYSTERY MELVIN???" said George and Harold in disbelief.

"...and make up a story where I defeat Captain Underpants and become the world's greatest superhero. And you better not make me look stupid, either!" Mr Melvin shouted.

"But we can't make a comic book right now," cried Harold. "We've gotta chase after Captain Kruppy the . . . uh . . . Underpants Kid."

"You can chase after him all you want," said Mr Melvin, "*AFTER* you make that comic book. Now get going! I've got a time machine to build."

CHAPTER 7

THE PURPLE POTTY

Mr Melvin went out and bought all the things he needed to build his time machine. Now he just needed a *place* to build it. He wanted someplace quiet and private. Someplace empty and secluded. A room that nobody ever, EVER used.

"I've got it!" he cried. "Our school library!"

The library at Jerome Horwitz Elementary
School had once been a wonderful place
of knowledge and learning. But a few years
back, the librarian, Miss Singerbrains, had
begun banning most of the books. Now
the library was filled only with rows of empty
bookshelves and posters that warned of
the potential subversive dangers of reading. It
was the perfect place to hatch an evil plan.

Mr Melvin pushed his cart into the dusty,
cobwebby room and flicked on the lights.

"Welcome, sir," said Miss Singerbrains. "Have you come to check out the book?"

"Uh, nooo," said Mr Melvin. "I need to find a large box, like a phone booth or something."

"There's a purple portable potty down in the basement," said Miss Singerbrains.

"That'll do," Mr Melvin said. "Go get it for me."

"I can't carry that thing up three flights of stairs all by myself," cried Miss Singerbrains.

"All right, all right," said Mr Melvin. "I'll help you."

Mr Melvin supervised while Miss Singerbrains carried the heavy potty to the top of the treacherous steps.

"Good job," said Mr Melvin. "Now go clean out your desk. You're fired."

"FIRED?!!?" cried Miss Singerbrains. "What for?"

"Uh . . . for the rest of your life," said Mr Melvin.

CHAPTER 8

MEANWHILE, BACK IN OUTER SPACE. . .

A team of scientists working at the Piqua Order of Professional Space and Interplanetary Explorers (POOPSIE) were on their way to investigate the planet Uranus, when they came across something that was very strange.

Major "Buzz" Tomski and his crew had just discovered a bizarre cluster of what appeared to be robots and toilets resting on the planet's surface.

The astronauts were so busy looking at their monitor that they didn't notice the three slimy, squishy, boogery thingies speeding towards their spaceship.

CHAPTER 9

GROUND CONTROL TO MAJOR TOMSKI

Suddenly, a very concerned voice came across the POOPSIE space phone. "What's going on up there, bub?" asked Ground Control.

"W-we're OK," said Major Tomski as he unzipped the cockpit's window screen for a better look. "But it appears our ship has just been splattered by three unidentified squishy objects!"

"That does it!" said Ground Control. "This mission is just getting too strange. I want you guys to turn that ship around and come on back home."

"Will do," said Major Tomski. He pushed in the clutch, shifted the ship into reverse, and in no time at all, the POOPSIE shuttle was headed back to Earth . . .

. . . with three giggling stowaways hanging on for the long ride home.

CHAPTER 10
MEAN MR MELVIN

The next day, Mr Melvin was putting the finishing touches on his time machine when he heard cries of laughter out in the hallway.

He opened the library door and saw a group of third graders happily reading George and Harold's newest comic book. Mr Melvin stomped down the hall, grabbed the comic out of their hands, and gasped in horror.

"WHAT THE —?!!?" he screamed as he glared at the comic book's cover.

CHAPTER 12
MAD MR MELVIN

Mr Melvin was furious. He marched into the office and turned on the school intercom.

"George Beard and Harold Hutchins," he shouted over the loudspeakers, "meet Mr Melv – er, I mean, Mr *Krupp* in the school library RIGHT NOW!"

"We have a library?" said George.

After about twenty minutes of searching, George and Harold finally came across a room they had never seen before. They entered cautiously, stepping quietly past rows and rows of empty bookshelves until they met up with Mr Melvin.

"I told you guys to give me a cool name and not to make me look stupid!" Mr Melvin screamed, clutching their comic book in his sweaty hand.

"Oops," said George. "I thought you said to give you a stupid name and NOT to make you look cool."

"Yeah," said Harold. "It was an honest misunderstanding."

Mr Melvin threw the comic book to the ground, then led George and Harold over to the Purple Potty.

"Remember when I had that great idea to build a time machine?" asked Mr Melvin.

"Actually," said George, "that was *my*—"

"Well, here it is," Mr Melvin interrupted triumphantly. "And you two smarty-pantses are going to test it out for me!"

"Huh?" said Harold.

"I'm sending you kids back in time to the day before yesterday," Mr Melvin said. "And you better not return until you've got my Combine-O-Tron 2000."

"Cool," said George. "I've always wanted to travel through time."

Mr Melvin had a great deal of instructions for George and Harold before they left on their journey. And though the instructions were quite boring, it would have benefited the boys if they had paid attention instead of switching the letters around on a nearby bulletin board.

Mr Melvin spoke at length about the workings of the time machine and the proper etiquette of time travel.

"You must be very careful that nobody sees you on your journey," Mr Melvin said. "If they do, just zap them with my new invention, the Forgetchamacallit 2000."

"This will erase everything in their short-term memory, and they won't remember ever seeing you." Mr Melvin had also built a fake Combine-O-Tron 2000 to switch with the real one.

Finally, Mr Melvin gave George and Harold a very important warning: "Whatever you do, it is very important that you don't use this time machine two days in a row. It needs to cool off *every other day*, or else it might open up an oppozo-dimensional reality rift that could destroy the entire planet."

George and Harold started laughing at their new message on the bulletin board.

"HEY!" Mr Melvin shouted. "Have you kids even heard *one* word I've said?"

"Yeah, yeah, yeah," said George. "We gotta switch the thing with the thingy!"

"And if somebody sees us," said Harold, "we'll zap 'em with the whichamajiggy."

"Don't worry, we *got* it!" said George.

George and Harold stepped into the
Purple Potty as Mr Melvin closed the door
behind them. Harold set the controller for
the day before yesterday. Then George
pulled the chain. Suddenly, there was a
brilliant flash of green light, and the Purple
Potty disappeared.

CHAPTER 13

THE DAY BEFORE
YESTERDAY

After a few moments of flashing lights,
everything became quiet. Harold opened the
potty door and peeked out into the darkened
library. Cautiously the two time travellers
stepped to the library window and looked out.
There they saw Melvin's father, Mr Sneedly,
zapping the Bionic Booger Boy with a blast
from the Combine-O-Tron 2000.

"Been there," said George.

"Done that," said Harold.

In the corner, George and Harold found a coat and hat, which belonged to Miss Singerbrains. Immediately, they thought of a plan. Harold put on the coat and hat, and climbed on to George's shoulders.

"I sure hope this disguise works," said Harold.

"It better," said George. "We can't risk letting them recognize us."

Soon George and Harold were at the scene of the action. Mr Sneedly had just fired the Combine-O-Tron 2000 a second time, and now the boys were ready to make their move.

"Um, excuse me, Mr Sneedly," said Harold, trying very hard to sound like a grown-up. "I'd like to present unto you *The Most Brilliantest Science Guy of the Whole Wide World Award*."

"Really?" cried Mr Sneedly. "It's always been my dream to win that award!"

"But first," said Harold, "I'd like to have a look at that Combine-O-Thingy."

"OK," said Mr. Sneedly. He handed Harold the Combine-O-Tron 2000 and smiled proudly.

"Um . . . " said Harold. "I need to look at it behind those bushes over there."

Harold and George wobbled over to the bushes, unbuttoned their coat and switched the two Combine-O-Trons. Then they wobbled back and handed the fake Combine-O-Tron 2000 to Mr Sneedly.

"Um . . . everything seems to be in order," said Harold. "But before we present the award, we'd like to get a photo of you."

"Who's *we*?" asked Mr Sneedly.

"Uh . . . I mean *I'd* like to get a photo of you," said Harold nervously.

George stuck his hand out of the coat and held up the Forgetchamacallit 2000.

"Say cheese," said Harold.

Mr Sneedly looked down in shock at George's hand. Then George pressed the button.

FLASH!

Suddenly, Mr Sneedly forgot everything
that had just happened. Dazed and confused,
he stumbled back and rejoined his wife just
in time for the Robo-Boogers to come to life
and smash the fake Combine-O-Tron 2000.

Meanwhile, George and Harold were running with all their might back to the library, carrying the *real* Combine-O-Tron 2000.

"That was SO easy!" laughed George.

"Yeah!" said Harold. "We sure got lucky this time!"

But when they reached the library door, George and Harold discovered that they hadn't been quite so lucky after all.

CHAPTER 14
MISS SINGERBRAINS

"What the heck is going on here?" shouted Miss Singerbrains. "I just got back from the restroom and found a *portable potty* in my library!"

"Harold!" said George. "Zap her with the Forgetcha-thingy – quick!"

"Nobody's zapping anybody with anything!" shouted Miss Singerbrains. She grabbed the Forgetchamacallit 2000 out of Harold's hands and yanked the Combine-O-Tron 2000 out of George's hands.

"I'm taking these things to the police right now!" she said. "Maybe they can sort this mess out!"

Miss Singerbrains marched downstairs
to the parking lot, got in her car, and began
driving to the police station.

"Well," said Harold, "we'll never catch up
with her now!"

"Sure we will!" said George. "All we need
are some *wings*!"

88

CHAPTER 15

65 MILLION YEARS BEFORE THE DAY BEFORE YESTERDAY

George and Harold grabbed a box of crackers off Miss Singerbrains's desk. Then the two friends stepped inside the Purple Potty and closed the door. Quickly, George reset the controls and pulled down on the chain.

A flash of green light lit up the room, and the Purple Potty vanished.

Suddenly, George and Harold were transported back in time to the late Cretaceous period of the Mesozoic era, a time when dinosaurs ruled the Earth.

Cautiously, George and Harold peeked out of the Purple Potty, which was now nestled precariously in the branches of a tall tree.

"Here chickie, chickie, chickie!" called George.

"Polly want a cracker?" called Harold as he tossed a handful of crackers into the air.

Suddenly, the two boys were swarmed by hungry pterodactyls.

Before long, a friendly-looking pterodactyl (a Quetzalcoatlus to be exact) swooped down and grabbed some crackers from Harold's hand.

"Aww, look," said Harold. "He likes me!"

"Great," said George. "Let's get him into the time machine and get out of here!"

Carefully, Harold took the pterodactyl in his arms and carried him into the Purple Potty. Then, the boys closed the door behind them, reset the controls, and pulled down on the chain.

Suddenly, George and Harold (and their new reptilian pal) were transported forward in time to the day before yesterday.

The door of the time machine swung open, and the three friends sailed out of the Purple Potty, through the library window, and up over the town.

George looked down on the city streets until finally he located Miss Singerbrains's car. "There she is!" George cried.

"I sure love our new pterodactyl," said Harold. "I'm gonna name him Crackers."

"Don't give him a name," said George. "We're not keeping him. We're just borrowing him!"

George, Harold and Crackers swooped down and landed on Miss Singerbrains's car, which was parked at a traffic light.

Miss Singerbrains screamed in horror.

"Wait!" cried George. "There's no reason to be afraid. You're just *dreaming*!"

"I'm dreaming?" asked Miss Singerbrains.

"Sure. Think about it," said Harold. "Purple Potties appearing out of nowhere . . . kids running around with laser zappers . . . pterosaurs landing on your car . . . this stuff only happens in dreams."

"Gosh, you're right," said Miss Singerbrains. "But it all seems so real."

"Well, trust us," said George. "In a few minutes you won't remember any of it."

Before long, George, Harold and Miss Singerbrains were all gliding back to school with their good pal Crackers. The Combine-O-Tron 2000 and the Forgetchamacallit 2000 were safe once again.

Soon, they arrived back at the library.

"I'll keep an eye on Miss Singerbrains," said George. "You take that pterodactyl back where we found him."

"Aww, can't we keep him?" asked Harold.

"No," said George sternly. "He belongs in his own time. Now take him back!"

"Aww, *maaaan*," said Harold.

Sadly, Harold carried Crackers into the
Purple Potty and closed the door. After a few
seconds, the time machine disappeared in
a flash of green light.

A half hour later, another flash of green light filled the room, and the Purple Potty was back.

"What took you so long?" asked George.

"Ummm . . . nothing," said Harold.

"Did you have any trouble taking Crackers back to his home?" asked George.

"Ummmm . . . not really," said Harold.

"You *DID* take him back to his home, didn't you?" asked George.

"Ummmmm . . . sure," said Harold, though he didn't *sound* very sure.

Quickly, George zapped Miss Singerbrains with the Forgetchamacallit 2000 and jumped into the Purple Potty. Then, with a quick flash of green light, they were gone.

CHAPTER 16
BACK TO THE PRESENT

Mr Melvin was very happy to see his Purple Potty return to him . . . and even happier to see his beloved Combine-O-Tron 2000.

"Now all I need," he said with a sneer, "is to find Captain Underpants."

Fortunately, Captain Underpants (who you'll probably remember looked just like Melvin Sneedly) wasn't too far away. *Unfortunately*, he had spent the last two days getting himself into trouble.

First, he started off by annoying some old ladies. Captain Underpants had been helping them cross the street when he heard a little girl crying for her kitten, which was stuck in a tree.

Captain Underpants rescued the kitty but forgot about the old ladies.

"Hey!" shouted one of the old ladies. "That flying kid just left us up here in this tree!"

"I'm gonna get that kid if it's the last thing I do!" said the other old lady.

Next, Captain Underpants was soaring above the football field when he encountered an unidentified flying object. It was made of brown leather and had white stitching on the side.

"Hmmm," said Captain Underpants. "This could be a dangerous UFO!" He grabbed it and flew down to the football field, where, oddly, the school's football team was having a big game.

"I don't want anybody to panic!" Captain Underpants shouted. "But I just captured this UFO. I'm going to take it to the moon, where it can be safely destroyed."

Suddenly, the players from the visiting team tackled Captain Underpants, which cost the home team fifty metres . . . and the game.

"That kid just made us lose our biggest game of the year!" shouted Mr Meaner.

"I'm gonna get that kid if it's the last thing I do," snarled the quarterback.

Finally, Captain Underpants got on the bad side of some skateboarders in the park. He had politely pointed out the *No Skateboarding* signs, but the skateboarders refused to go away. So Captain Underpants had no choice but to snap their skateboards in half with his kung-fu kicking action.

Then it was spankings for everyone!

"Dude!" cried one of the skateboarders. "That little dude just, like, duded our dudeboards."

"Dude," said another skateboarder. "I'm gonna dude that dude if it's the last dude I dude!"

CHAPTER 17

THE BIG SWITCHEROONIE

Mr Melvin ordered George and Harold to stick their heads out the window and call for Captain Underpants. Soon, the Waistband Warrior appeared.

Mr Melvin welcomed the caped hero inside and asked him to pose for a photo.

"Why, I'd be delighted," said Captain Underpants.

"Great," said Mr Melvin. "Put these clothes on and stand over there!"

At first, Captain Underpants was reluctant
to put on clothes, but he finally agreed.

Mr Melvin, who had worked all afternoon
reconfiguring the Combine-O-Tron 2000,
pressed the start button, then ran and stood
beside Captain Underpants. Suddenly, two
glowing lasers began encoding the DNA of
the two subjects it was about to combine.

Then, a burst of brilliant grey light shot out of the Combine-O-Tron 2000 and formed a ball of energy between Captain Underpants and Mr Melvin. They both slid together into the grey light and formed a giant glob of fleshy goo.

The newly reconfigured Combine-O-Tron 2000 then switched polarities and began the process of separating the two human elements. The grey ball of light slowly changed to a lovely shade of pink.

Suddenly, there was a blinding flash of light, a quick puff of smoke, and it was all over. Everybody's brains were back where they belonged.

"Wow, that sure is a weird camera," said Captain Underpants (who now looked exactly like Captain Underpants). "Can I take these clothes off now? They're bad for my image."

"Go right ahead," said Melvin Sneedly (who now looked exactly like Melvin Sneedly).

Finally, it looked as if everything was back to normal. But as we all know, looks can be deceiving.

CHAPTER 18

THE RETURN OF THE RIDICULOUS ROBO-BOOGERS

Just then, the POOPSIE space shuttle landed at Piqua International Airport. It wasn't the smoothest of landings, due to the fact that three robotic boogers had just eaten most of the shuttle's tailfin and nearly all of its rocket thrusters.

Major Tomski and his crew had barely escaped with their lives.

Inside the school library, Captain
Underpants heard the astronauts' panicked
cries coming from the airport.

"This looks like a job for me!" he shouted.
And with a mighty "Tra-La-Laaaaa!", he
leaped out the window . . .

. . . and fell three storeys to the ground.

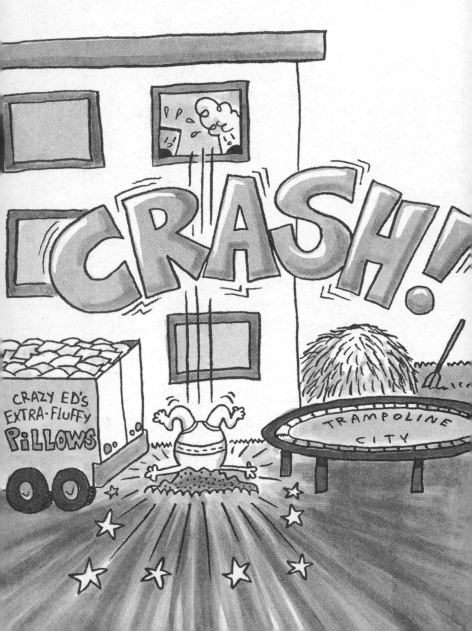

George and Harold screamed and ran downstairs.

"Captain Underpants!" cried George. "Are you OK?"

"Speak to us!" cried Harold.

Captain Underpants slowly lifted his head in confusion.

"Mummy . . ." he said weakly, ". . . my train went swimming in the piano."

Meanwhile, over at Piqua International
Airport, Carl, Trixie and Frankenbooger had
just finished eating the space shuttle and
were now starting to munch on the control
tower. The three globby gluttons grew bigger
and bigger with every enormous bite.

"C'mon, Captain Underpants," cried George. "You've gotta save those people!"

"But I forgot how to fly," Captain Underpants said sheepishly.

"You didn't forget," laughed Melvin Sneedly, who was now floating above their heads. "You've just LOST your super powers. But don't worry, they've been safely transferred into *MY* body. Now *I'm* the world's greatest superhero!"

"Melvin," cried George, "those Robo-Boogers came back to Earth! They're attacking people at the airport! You've gotta help those people!"

"I'm not doing a thing until you guys change that comic book!" Melvin said. "And you better make me look cool this time!"

"But there's no time," cried Harold. "Those people need your help NOW!"

"Well, you better start drawing then, art boy!" said Melvin.

CHAPTER 19

NEVER UNDERESTIMATE THE POWER OF UNDERWEAR

George and Harold begged Melvin to use his super powers to save the day, but Melvin continued to refuse. Finally, Captain Underpants stepped in.

"You may have taken away my super powers," the Waistband Warrior said, "but I still have the power of underwear on my side. And nobody can take that away from me!"

Captain Underpants turned and ran towards the airport.

"Melvin," cried George frantically, "if you don't do something, those boogers are gonna *kill* Mr Krupp!"

"That's not *my* fault," said Melvin. "You're the ones who wrote that stupid comic book about me. Now change it, or ELSE!"

George and Harold looked at each other. Their choice was simple: either fight with Captain Underpants (and probably die), or give in to the dark side and live.

The two boys turned and ran to the airport.

CHAPTER 20
BOOGER BRUNCH

George and Harold quickly caught up with
Captain Underpants. Soon, they were all at
the airport witnessing the carnage of the
Ridiculous Robo-Boogers.

Captain Underpants shouted out
a triumphant "Tra-La-Laaaaa!" from below.
Suddenly, the three Robo-Boogers turned
towards the familiar-sounding voice. Quickly,
their laser-guided eyeballs zoomed in on
three of the heroes who had made their lives
so miserable back in chapter 1. Immediately,
the Robo-Boogers leaped at George, Harold
and Captain Underpants . . . and the chase
was on . . . again!

CHAPTER 21
CORNERED

The Robo-Boogers continued chasing George, Harold and Captain Underpants, until at last the three frightened friends were cornered at a local shopping centre.

In a desperate attempt to save themselves, the three brave heroes began taking items from the outside sales bins and throwing them at the snarling beasts.

George grabbed a pair of low-fat tennis shoes and tossed them at Trixie. Trixie gobbled them up.

Harold found a delicious tube of wild-cherry-flavored haemorrhoid ointment and flung it at Frankenbooger.

Frankenbooger swallowed it whole.

Captain Underpants picked up a
genetically-modified, organic-orange-
flavoured orange and chucked it at Carl.
Carl chewed it up with a smug grin.

Suddenly, Carl's laser eyes grew incredibly large. The haughty smile on his face turned into a panicked gasp as the wet, gooshy snot that covered his body began to dry up and crumble. Huge, crispy booglets shot off his smouldering robotic endoskeleton like green popcorn.

"What's going on?" cried Harold.

"It's the *oranges*!" cried George. "It's gotta be the vitamin C in these oranges. It's combatting the cold and flu that caused those boogers to turn evil!"

Carl thrashed around brutally as more and
more of his disintegrating body cracked off
and fell to the ground. Finally, the lights in
his panic-stricken laser eyes slowly went
out. He stumbled over and crashed horribly
into the parking lot. Carl – was dead.

CHAPTER 22
VITAMIN C YOU LATER

George, Harold and Captain Underpants quickly began chucking oranges at Trixie and Frankenbooger. But the two remaining Robo-Boogers had got wise to the power of vitamin C. They ducked, jumped, dodged and darted, doing whatever they could to avoid being hit by the deadly oranges.

"Hey! I've got an idea," said Captain Underpants. He grabbed two crates of oranges and ran off, while George and Harold continued flinging fruit ferociously.

"Where does he think *he's* going?" said George.

"I don't know," said Harold, "but his idea better work. We're running out of oranges!"

Soon, George and Harold were down to their last two oranges. They threw them as hard as they could, but alas, the potent projectiles missed their terrifying targets.

Trixie and Frankenbooger grabbed George and Harold and dangled them above their gigantic mouths.

"Well," said George, "it looks like this is the end."

"Yep," said Harold. "It was nice knowing you, pal."

Suddenly, the Robo-Boogers heard a familiar "Tra-La-Laaaaa!" coming from somewhere over on the next page.

The repulsive Robo-Boogers dropped George and Harold, and stomped over to page 130. There they found Captain Underpants standing at the top of a large novelty toilet on the roof of John's House of Toilets. He was shouting, "Tra-La-Laaaaa!" and doing a very annoying dance, which made the Robo-Boogers very, very angry.

JOHN'S
HOUSE OF
TOILETS

We'll
Bowl
You
Over!

CHAPTER 23

THE UNDERPANTS DANCE
(IN FLIP-O-RAMA™)

You've tried the Twist,
mastered the Macarena,
and figured out
the Funky Chicken. . .

Now it's time to learn the most
annoying dance ever:
the Underpants Dance.

It's sure to irritate parents,
teachers, evil villains
and kids of all ages!

Just follow the easy steps
in this chapter, and learn
the Underpants Dance today!!!

PILKEY® BRAND

O-RAMA

HERE'S HOW IT WORKS!

STEP 1

First, place your *left* hand inside the dotted lines marked "LEFT HAND HERE". Hold the book open *flat*.

STEP 2

Grasp the *right-hand* page with your right thumb and index finger (inside the dotted lines marked "RIGHT THUMB HERE").

STEP 3

Now *quickly* flip the right-hand page back and forth until the picture appears to be *animated*.

FLIP-O-RAMA 1

(pages 135 and 137)

Remember, flip *only* page 135.
While you are flipping, be sure you
can see the picture on page 135
and the one on page 137.
If you flip quickly, the two
pictures will start to look like
<u>one</u> *animated* picture.

For extra fun, try humming
a stupid song and flipping to the beat!

LEFT HAND HERE

STEP 1:
THE WEDGIE
WIGGLE

135

RIGHT THUMB HERE

136

STEP 1:
THE WEDGIE
WIGGLE

FLIP-O-RAMA 2

(pages 139 and 141)

Remember, flip *only* page 139.
While you are flipping, be sure you
can see the picture on page 139
and the one on page 141.
If you flip quickly, the two
pictures will start to look like
<u>one</u> *animated* picture.

For extra fun, try humming
a stupid song and flipping to the beat!

LEFT HAND HERE

STEP 2:
THE TOILET-TOP
TANGO

RIGHT
THUMB
HERE

STEP 2:
THE TOILET-TOP
TANGO

FLIP-O-RAMA 3

(pages 143 and 145)

Remember, flip *only* page 143.
While you are flipping, be sure you
can see the picture on page 143
and the one on page 145.
If you flip quickly, the two
pictures will start to look like
<u>one</u> *animated* picture.

For extra fun, try humming
a stupid song and flipping to the beat!

LEFT HAND HERE

STEP 3:
THE WAISTBAND
WATUSI

143

STEP 3:
THE WAISTBAND
WATUSI

FLIP-O-RAMA 4

(pages 147 and 149)

Remember, flip *only* page 147.
While you are flipping, be sure you
can see the picture on page 147
and the one on page 149.
If you flip quickly, the two
pictures will start to look like
<u>one</u> *animated* picture.

For extra fun, try humming
a stupid song and flipping to the beat!

LEFT HAND HERE

STEP 4:
THE BIG BUTT
BOOGIE

RIGHT
THUMB
HERE

148

STEP 4:
THE BIG BUTT
BOOGIE

CHAPTER 24
SQUISHIES, PART 2

Trixie and Frankenbooger had seen enough.
They couldn't stand to watch Captain
Underpants doing that stupid dance one
second longer. So they pushed down on
the seat of the large novelty toilet to hoist
themselves up on the roof.

Unfortunately for Trixie and Frankenbooger, they had been so irritated by the Underpants Dance that they hadn't noticed the two crates of oranges placed carefully under the gigantic toilet seat. When they pressed down, the pressure of the toilet seat crushed the orange crates, spraying delicious, vitaminey orange juice all over their big, bad, boogery bodies.

George, Harold, and Captain Underpants watched as their monstrous archenemies began decomposing before their very eyes.

"What happened to them?" asked Harold.

"I gave them a *Squishy*," said Captain Underpants. "It's the latest fad."

The Robo-Boogers jerked around wildly
as the quickly drying snot crumbled off of
their smoking robotic endoskeletons. Then,
after a few minutes of spinning and
screaming, they slowly tumbled to the
ground in two metallic heaps.

Trixie and Frankenbooger — were dead.

CHAPTER 25
"BIG MELVIN"

Soon, Ingrid Ashley from Channel 4
Eyewitness News arrived at the scene.
"How did you manage to destroy the Robo-
Boogers?" she asked.

"I'll answer that," said Melvin Sneedly, as
he swooped in front of the cameras. He was
robed in some old drapes that he had tied
around his neck at the last minute, and he
looked quite silly.

"I, *Big Melvin*, fought those monsters
with my mighty super powers," Melvin fibbed.
"Then I destroyed them with my super-smart
brain!"

"No, you didn't," said Harold.

"You weren't even here!" said George.

"Don't listen to those guys," said Melvin. "I, *Big Melvin*, am the real hero here." Melvin flew above the two defeated Robo-Boogers and used his new laser eye-beams to burn the letters *B* and *M* in front of the dead creatures.

"Just like Zorro," said Big Melvin, "I shall sign my initials on all of my heroic handiwork. From now on, whenever you see a big *BM*, you'll think of me!"

"That's funny," said George. "Big *BM*s have always made me think of you."

Big Melvin flew over to Captain
Underpants and grabbed him by the arm.

"Now," said Big Melvin, "the entire world
shall bear witness to the humiliating defeat
of Captain Underpants!"

Suddenly, George and Harold got an idea.
They turned and ran back to the school while
Big Melvin continued to threaten Captain
Underpants.

"I command you to bow down to me,"
shouted Big Melvin.

"*Never!*" said Captain Underpants.

"You SHALL bow down to me!" Big
Melvin yelled.

"*I SHAN'T!*" cried Captain Underpants.

"Then," said Big Melvin, as he untied the
drapes around his neck, "you will feel the
power of my wrath!"

CHAPTER 26

THE DRAPES OF WRATH

Big Melvin held his drapes tightly, then smacked Captain Underpants in the tushie with them.

"I command you to deny underwear and accept the power of Big Melvin!" he shouted.

"No *way, Pedro*!" cried Captain Underpants.

Big Melvin smacked Captain Underpants again.

"Bow down to me," he commanded, "and
I shall spare your life!"

"Aww, go jump off a duck!" said Captain
Underpants defiantly.

Suddenly, George and Harold returned to the scene, out of breath, and hiding something behind their backs.

"Hey, Big Melvin!" shouted George, huffing and puffing.

"What?" yelled Big Melvin.

Harold pulled the Combine-O-Tron 2000 out from behind his back and aimed it at Melvin and Captain Underpants.

"You shouldn't leave your toys lyin' around in the library, bub!" he said slyly.

Melvin shrieked in horror as Harold pulled the trigger.

BLAZZZZT!

A blinding flash of grey light shot out of the Combine-O-Tron 2000, surrounding Melvin and Captain Underpants and squishing them together.

George had reset the controller to combine them both, transfer the super powers back to Captain Underpants, then separate them.

"I sure hope this works," said Harold.

"Me, too," said George.

CHAPTER 27

TO MAKE A LONG STORY SHORT

It did.

CHAPTER 28

WITH BIG UNDERWEAR COMES BIG RESPONSIBILITY

Big Melvin fell to the ground with a thud. Immediately, Captain Underpants began floating in the air.

"Hey!" cried the good Captain. "I've got my super powers back! I knew that underwear would never let me down!"

George turned and zapped the Channel 4 Eyewitness News team with the Forgetchamacallit 2000.

FLASH!

Suddenly, the Channel 4 Eyewitness News team (as well as everyone at home watching the story unfold on Channel 4 Eyewitness News) immediately forgot what had just happened.

The horror was over, everything was back to normal, and everyone was happy.

Well . . . everyone except Big Melvin, that is.

"*Waaaaaah!*" sobbed Melvin. "I want my
super powers back!"

"Aww, quit your whining, bub!" said
George. "You've been a total jerk for the last
two books. You should just be happy that
you didn't get your comeuppance!"

CHAPTER 29

COMEUPPANCE
SEE ME SOMETIME

Soon, a crowd gathered and began to recognize Melvin.

"Hey!" cried Miss Anthrope. "That's the little squirt who said he was going to *fire* me!"

"There he is!" shouted a couple of very angry old ladies. "That's the little brat who left us up in a tree."

"He made us lose the big game," cried the entire football team simultaneously.

"Dudes," yelled one of the skateboarders, "that's the little dude who duded our dudeboards a few dudes ago!"

"Heh, heh," laughed Melvin nervously. "Maybe I'll just go home now."

"*Get him!*" shouted the old ladies.

"AAAAAH!" screamed Melvin as he ran away, followed closely by a large group of very angry people.

CHAPTER 30
HAROLD'S SURPRISE

As Melvin and his angry mob ran off into
the sunset, George and Harold had just
one last thing to deal with.

A quick squirt of water to Captain
Underpants's face was all it took to bring
him back to his Kruppy old self.

"Well, that takes care of that," said
George, and the two boys walked back
to their tree house.

As George climbed up the ladder to the
tree house, Harold became quite fidgety.

"Ummmmmm . . . " said Harold nervously,
"there's something I should probably tell
you, George."

But when George reached the top of
the ladder and looked inside the tree house,
no explanation was necessary.

"Hey!" said George. "I thought you told me you took Crackers back to his home."

"I did," said Harold. "Back to his *new* home."

"*Harold*," said George sternly, "we can't keep a pet pterodactyl. Do you know how many crackers they need to eat every day? We could never afford it."

"I know. . ." said Harold sadly. "But look how cute he is. And he's made friends with Sulu, too. Can't we keep him for just one night?"

"Well, all right," said George. "But we're taking him back tomorrow."

CHAPTER 31

TOMORROW

The next day, George, Harold and Sulu
returned to school with Crackers tucked
snugly into Harold's book bag. Together, the
four friends sneaked back upstairs to the
library, where the Purple Potty stood before
them in all its forbidden glory.

"Come on," said George. "Let's give this
baby another spin."

"I don't know," said Harold. "Maybe
we should give it a day to cool off."

"Nah, I'm sure it can be used two
days in a row," said George. "What
could possibly go wrong?"

"But didn't Melvin warn us not to use this machine two days in a row?" asked Harold.

"Yeah," said George. "Back in chapter 12, starting with the first word in the third line of the second paragraph on page 77."

"What exactly did he say?" asked Harold.

"Beats me," said George. "I'm not very good at remembering details."

"Well, I don't know about this," said Harold. "What if our journey brings about the end of the world as we know it?"

"That's ridiculous," said George. "It all sounds like a set-up for the sequel to a really lame children's book!"

The four friends stepped inside the Purple
Potty and closed the door behind them.
George set the controller to return them to
the Cretaceous period of the Mesozoic era
and then pulled the chain.

Suddenly, an orange light began flashing
wildly.

"Hey! I don't remember seeing an orange
light before," said Harold.

Then the Purple Potty began to shake
and rock violently.

"I don't remember this thing shaking
and rocking before, either," said George.

"Something is wrong!" cried Harold.
"Something is terribly, *terribly* wrong!"

Suddenly, the entire room lit up with an explosive burst of lightning, and the Purple Potty began to disappear into a whirlwind of electric air.

The only thing that could be heard above the chaotic clatter was the sound of two terrified voices screaming into the unknown abyss.

"Oh, NO!" screamed one of the voices.

"HERE WE GO AGAIN!" screamed the other.